HASBRO and its logo, SONGBIRD SERENADE, MY LITTLE PONY, and all related characters are trademarks of Hasbro and are used with permission. © 2018 Hasbro. All Rights Reserved. MY LITTLE PONY: THE MOVIE © 2017 My Little Pony Productions, LLC.

Cover design by Ching N. Chan. Cover illustration by Tony Fleecs.

Little, Brown and Company
Hachette Book Group
1290 Avenue of the Americas, New York, NY 10104
Visit us at LBYR.com
mylittlepony.com

First Edition: January 2018

Little, Brown and Company is a division of Hachette Book Group, Inc. The Little, Brown name and logo are trademarks of Hachette Book Group, Inc.

The publisher is not responsible for websites (or their content) that are not owned by the publisher.

Library of Congress Control Number 2017954742

ISBNs: 978-0-316-55747-4 (paper over board), 978-0-316-55745-0 (ebook)

Printed in the United States of America

LSC-H

10 9 8 7 6 5 4 3 2 1

BEYOND EQUESTRIA

PINKIE PIE STEPS UP

G.M. Berrow

Little, Brown and Company
New York • Boston

CHAPTER ONE

The Crystaller Building sparkled in the midday sunshine, as if the rows of skyscrapers flanking it were spires in a glittering royal crown. As the Manehattan skyline rushed past the window, Pinkie Pie felt a fizzy, bubbly rush of excitement inside of her. Even though she'd visited many times before, she'd always found the big city impressive. There were so many fascinating things to discover within its confines. Manehattan was like a gigantic shiny treasure trove filled with tasty treats, awe-inspiring sights, and interesting ponies to befriend. The city was always buzzing with a nonstop flurry of motion—like a big party that everypony was invited to. It was no wonder Pinkie Pie liked visiting so much.

"We're almost to the station!" Pinkie Pie squealed, loud enough for the other ponies in the train car to join in on her delight. A few of them gave a courteous nod to acknowledge that they'd heard her. The rest of the passengers remained serious. They were too busy reading their copies of the *Canterlot Gazette* or dozing off.

"Don't take it personally if they ignore you, dear," whispered an old Unicorn mare in a floppy green hat. She sat in the seat across from Pinkie Pie, using her magic to carefully knit another floppy green hat.

"Oh, I don't," Pinkie Pie chirped in response.

"They're just commuters." The old mare nodded as she set down her knitting and began to search through her knitted, oversize bag. She adjusted her glasses and looked up at Pinkie. "Do you work in the city?"

The pink pony shook her curly fuchsia mane. "No, ma'am." Pinkie Pie pulled an orange envelope out of her saddlebag and held it up. Bits of rainbow-colored confetti fell out onto the train seat. "But I am meeting a friend who wants to hire me for a job."

"How lovely." The old mare popped a candy into her mouth and held out her hoof to Pinkie Pie. "Butterscotch?"

"Nope, his name is *Cheese Sandwich*." Pinkie giggled. "He's my party-planning pal. I can't wait to see him again and see what party he's planning to plan!" The scenery outside disappeared as the train chugged into the darkened tunnel of Maneway Station. Pinkie sprang to her hooves and trotted to the doors. As the bell whistled and the doors opened, Pinkie gave one last wave to her friendly seatmate. "Goodbye, train, and *helloooo*, Manehattan!"

"Have fun, dear," replied the old mare with a nod and a chuckle.

"Oh, don't worry—I always do!" Pinkie called over her shoulder, and burst out into the bustling station with a huge smile on her face. The impending excitement of seeing her old friend again filled Pinkie with energy. She bounded across the marble floors even quicker than usual, whistling a happy tune and darting with ease through the crowds of tourist ponies, locals, and serious commuters.

Twenty blocks later, Pinkie Pie finally caught sight of her destination: Hay's Pizza. It was the home of the best slice in town and the location of her very special meeting. Pinkie's tummy grumbled when the delicious smells of pizza hit her muzzle.

A bell jangled from the doorknob as Pinkie Pie pushed her way into the restaurant. Hay's Pizza was packed with the lunchtime crowd: customers busy chomping down on cheesy slices and chatting about important city-pony topics. Pinkie instantly felt pretty cool—this time, she was one of them, here on Top Secret Party Business.

Pinkie scanned the tables. She recognized

two ponies from back in Ponyville, Lyra and Bon Bon, sharing a pizza at a table in the corner. They turned to look at her, but then quickly went back to their lunch. There was no sign of Cheese Sandwich, so Pinkie Pie trotted over to the counter to double-check. Maybe he was seated in the back.

"Excuse me, mister!" Pinkie chirped. "Have you seen Cheese?"

The gruff stallion behind the counter turned to the pink pony with a raised brow. "What d'ya want, kid?" he asked as he wiped his flour-dusted hooves on his apron, which was already covered in grease and tomato stains.

"I was just wondering if you had any tables reserved under 'Cheese'? Or 'Pie'? Or perhaps... 'Cheese Pie'?"

"Two slices of cheese pie, comin' right up!"

The stallion grunted, slapped two enormous pieces of pizza on a plate, and slid it over to Pinkie. "That'll be two bits." Pinkie chuckled at the mistake and tossed him the coins. She took her accidental pizza and sat down near the front window to wait. Pinkie hoped she'd gotten the day right.

"Geroooooonimoooooo!" A huge blast of confetti shaped like mushrooms, olives, and other pizza toppings erupted from the open front door. The confetti rained down onto the confused customers as none other than Cheese Sandwich himself burst through the cloud of colors!

"Cheese!" cheered Pinkie Pie as she sprang up to give him a hug.

"Pinkie Pie!" he shouted back, and the two ponies took a seat.

He looked exactly the same as the last time

Pinkie Pie had seen him—tall and gangly with a curly brown mane, and a gigantic toothy grin on his face. The only difference was that today his shirt was patterned with hundreds of tiny pineapples instead of his usual yellow one. He clearly agreed that pineapple and pizza went well together.

"Okay, let's not skip around the shrubbery." Cheese Sandwich put his hooves on the table. "I need you to help me plan the wackiest, wild-est, *wow-wow-wowie-est* party that Manehattan's ever seen"—he looked around to make sure nopony was listening, then leaned across the table and whispered—"for the biggest stars in all Equestria!"

Pinkie Pie gasped. "You don't mean—"

"That's right!" Cheese laughed and nodded his head. "You and I are going to throw the

Pony Popstravaganza!" Pinkie Pie's eyes grew wide. She couldn't believe it. Pinkie had been hearing about the event for years from Rarity (who read about it in her magazines). The Pony Popstravaganza was supposedly the party to rival all parties—a big blowout to celebrate the very special nominees of the Glammy Awards.

"Wooo-hoooo!" Pinkie Pie cheered. "That's the best party ever!" She sprang up and did an excited twirl, much to the chagrin of their table neighbors. "We have so much to do!" she squealed. Pinkie Pie paced across the restaurant as she began to brainstorm.

"We'll need balloons. Tons of 'em. Balloon it up! We'll need confetti in every color of the rainbow, even colors that haven't been invented yet! Party hats! *ALL THE PARTY HATS!* I have to go back to Ponyville and—"

"*Uhhh*, Pinkie?" Cheese Sandwich gave a nervous smile and looked at the floor. "I don't think there's time for that—"

"Who doesn't have time for party hats?!"

"Nopony I want to know!" Cheese Sandwich laughed. "But what I was trying to say was...the party is tomorrow."

"Tomorrow?! Then we better eat these cheesy slices fast, Cheese!" Pinkie plopped back down on her chair, eyes wild. Before she could take a bite, Cheese reached across the table and picked up a slice. Then he turned it over and slapped it on top of the other one. He smiled proudly. "Now you've got a cheese sandwich to go!"

"Perfect! Because it's *go time*." Pinkie Pie took a massive bite. "Come on, Cheese!" Pinkie shouted as she made for the door, pizza sandwich in hoof. This had to be the coolest party they had ever planned, because if the Pony Popstravaganza wasn't the most spectacular soiree, Pinkie Pie and Cheese Sandwich might as well forget about planning another party in Manehattan ever again.

CHAPTER TWO

The next day had gone by with a whirly-twirly whoosh and a busy-dizzy blur. Since their meeting at Hay's Pizza, Pinkie Pie and Cheese Sandwich had worked tirelessly to put on the party of their lives. They'd rushed around the city, finding every streamer and balloon, and every star-shaped decoration in all Manehattan so the main ballroom of the Foal Seasons Hotel could be transformed into a star-studded wonderland for the big event. There were just a few hours to go till showtime.

Pinkie Pie had just finished securing the second set of star swings from the ceiling when Cheese Sandwich rolled in a gigantic fish tank. It was almost the size of Cheese's famous portable party-fruit-punch lake. "*Oooh!* Pretty!" Pinkie chirped. She climbed down her ladder and bounded over. "What's it for?"

"It's a starfish petting zoo scuba tank." Cheese pointed to the colorful rainbow of starfish stuck to the rocks inside. "So the party guests can dive right in and get the full star experience," he explained. "Trust me, it's gonna be a hit!"

"Brilliant idea, Cheese!" Pinkie praised as she dipped her hoof inside the tank to pet a purple starfish. It felt bumpy and a bit squishy. How silly and fun! Pinkie was almost sure none of the previous Pony Popstravaganza's party planners had ever thought of something so creative. "We really pulled this party together, didn't we?"

"We go together like melted cheese and toasted bread, Pinkie." Cheese Sandwich nodded. "We're the best team!" The two ponies stepped back and admired their work. Between the sculptures of each nominee made entirely out of fresh starfruit, the sparkling star swing, and now the epic starfish touch tank, it was more than just a sight to behold—it was a magnificent masterpiece of festive fun! Pinkie nodded, unable to contain her enthusiasm. "Do you think the super-duper important and famous pop ponies will like it?"

"If they don't love it, then my name isn't Cheese Sandwich."

As nighttime fell over Manehattan, hundreds of sparkling stars began to appear in the sky, adding to Pinkie and Cheese's brilliant theme. "Good thing I ordered clear skies from the Pegasi for tonight!" Pinkie said, patting herself on the back. Pinkie and Cheese were ready to go! They trotted over and took their place outside the main ballroom, next to the pink carpet, eagerly awaiting the arrival of their guests.

One by one, taxicabs and carriages began to pull up to the curb.

The door of a yellow taxi opened, and a pair of mares in long glittering evening gowns stepped out. Their manes were pinned into classic twists, and they smelled like delicate floral perfume. They had clearly spent all day primping for the soiree.

"All right, par-tay ponies!" Cheese shouted at the fancy ponies, waving his hooves in the air. He was wearing a shirt covered in rainbow stars, star-shaped sunglasses, and a hat covered in twinkly lights. Cheese was glowing so brightly that he was practically a spotlight, guiding the guests right to the party. "Let's get this thing *star*-ted!"

"Welcome to the Pony Popstravaganza! It's going to be stellar, startastic, and supernova-riffic!" promised Pinkie Pie. She tried to nod, but found it difficult to do so through the giant foam star-shaped costume she was wearing. The two fancy mares looked at Pinkie Pie, then back at each other and scrunched up their

muzzles in distaste. Then they trotted right past Pinkie and Cheese, talking in hushed whispers. Cheese Sandwich's face fell in disappointment. He began to shuffle around. Pinkie could tell her friend was especially nervous because he was back in his hometown. Making a good impression was very important.

"They must be so captivated with the decorations that they're already speechless," Pinkie suggested hopefully. She pointed her hoof at the starry arch of balloons and twinkling lights in the entryway.

"Melted Jarlsberg!" Cheese exclaimed with a satisfied smile. His brown mane bounced as he nodded. "That *must* be it."

A string of carriages pulled up, and each pony who arrived seemed to be more famous than the last. First Sapphire Shores and her entourage made a bold entrance. Next were Daisy Chain, Jewel Tone, Feather Bangs, and Moonlight Melody. Then came Songbird Serenade and her shy assistant, Crownpiece, who greeted Pinkie Pie and Cheese Sandwich with kind smiles. Songbird waltzed in and Crownpiece shuffled after her, dragging a large trunk on wheels that probably contained some sort of outfit change inside.

Finally, the last Glammy nominee, Countess Coloratura, had made her grand entrance in a glittering cream-colored shift gown and impossibly sparkly earrings. Ever since she'd gotten rid of her old manager, Svengallop, her look had gone from eccentric to light and refreshing. But Rara still knew how to make a statement when she wanted to, of course.

By the time the countess and her posse had

filed inside, the Foal Seasons was bursting with famous, sophisticated ponies. Since most of the guests were part of the fashion and music industries, it was not too surprising that they had all dressed themselves to the nines in designer fashion. Pinkie Pie didn't know too much about fashion, but she definitely recognized more than a few of Rarity's creations among the crowd. She couldn't wait to run into one of her best friends and see what other fun things were going to happen that night.

"Are you ready to rock, Roquefort?" Cheese Sandwich nudged Pinkie.

"You bet your Brie!" Pinkie replied. She bounced inside after her friend, feeling energized in a way that only a super-fun celebration could inspire. But the second that Pinkie Pie entered the party, her heart sank.

The star swings weren't swinging, the star-fruit sculptures were snubbed, and not a single pony was petting a starfish. The whole venue was packed to the brim with guests, but somehow nopony was doing anything except... *frowning*?

Cheese Sandwich galloped over, eyes wide. "This is *not* Gouda. This is bad-a! Pinkie... what are we gonna do?!"

CHAPTER THREE

Cheese Sandwich had never, in all his party-
planning days, seen such a monumental
flop of a fiesta right from the get-go. "If...
if...nopony has fun at the biggest party of the
year, our reputation as super party ponies will
be stinkier than a slab of Stilton!" He dove into
his giant rainbow-patterned saddlebag.

"I must have something in my bag of tricks
to liven this thing up...." Cheese pulled out a

rubber chicken labeled with the number two. "Oh, that's where you've been, Boneless Two. Any ideas, buddy?" He threw the chicken onto his back and continued to search for anything that might kick things up a notch or twenty.

At first, Pinkie Pie thought Cheese was overreacting a little bit. But as she began to stride past the fancy ponies, it became clear that most of them were practically falling asleep with snooty boredom.

"Yuck, the star theme is *so* overdone," said a mare with a fiery-red mane and a sour face. Her name was Ritzy Rose—the most famous lounge singer in the whole city. And she loved to constantly remind everypony of that fact. She waved her polished hoof in dismissal. "It's like—we *get it*, we're *stars*."

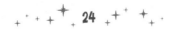

Jewel Tone, a fellow singer who was renowned for her impressive vocal range, nodded in agreement as she took a sip of her sparkling cider. "They could have at least had it at the observatory or something. Perhaps a 'Nightmare Moon' theme would have been a bit more original than this tired shtick."

Ritzy Rose rolled her eyes. "I wish *I* were exiled to the moon right now with how awful this party is!" The two ponies laughed and shook their heads at their surroundings, then blushed when they noticed Pinkie Pie eavesdropping nearby. They shot her fake smiles and went back to talking in hushed whispers.

"Pinkie Pie!" Rarity called out as she rushed over in a panic. "You have to do something. I just heard Moonlight Melody say she is going to...*leave*!" Rarity whimpered. "If she leaves, it's only a matter of time before more guests depart."

"I can't let that happen to Cheese! Manehattan is his hometown. He needs this party to be a hit!" Pinkie narrowed her eyes in determination. "I'm all over it—like whipped cream on a banana split," Pinkie assured. She furrowed her brow and rubbed her chin as she looked around the room. What was this party lacking?

Ponies were chatting with one another, but the place was surprisingly quiet... *too* quiet. That was it! Pinkie stomped her hoof on the ground in delight. "We need music!" exclaimed Pinkie Pie. "These are musical ponies—they just need to shake their flanks to some funky tunes!"

It was time to bring out the big party cannons. Pinkie Pie whistled and signaled a series of elaborate hoof motions to the corner, where the ten-piece pony band was just finishing setting up their equipment for later. They nodded back at her and struck up a jaunty song. *That should do the trick*, thought Pinkie, growing smug as a few ponies began to nod their heads to the beat. Pinkie caught Cheese's eye from across the room, and gave him two hooves up. He momentarily stopped juggling starfruits and smiled with relief.

The band's upbeat rendition of "Fly Mare to the Moon" was in full swing, but the dance floor was still empty. Maybe nopony wanted to be the first one out. Pinkie Pie bounced to the center and started swaying in time to the rhythm. Her fuchsia mane bopped up and down to the funky music. DJ Pon-3 joined in on her turntables, dropping the beat. It was so much fun that Pinkie Pie forgot all about trying to impress everypony!

She spun around, leaped across the floor, and kicked her legs out to the sides, back and forth.

Finally, the sleepy crowd began to take notice of Pinkie's sweet moves. They formed a curious circle around the dance floor and cheered as she shook her tail and did the "running pony."

"Come on, everypony!" Cheese Sandwich encouraged the partygoers. "Get your groove on like Pinkie Pie!"

The two ponies from Ponyville whom Pinkie Pie had seen at the pizza joint the day before, Lyra Heartstrings and Bon Bon, darted out to the dance floor. They joined in and copied Pinkie's moves.

"What are you guys doing here in Manehattan?!" Pinkie shouted over the music. "I saw you at the pizza place! Are you following me or something?" She laughed.

"What?!" Lyra shouted.

"*Ummm*...no! Of course not! We convinced Cheese Sandwich to get us on the guest list because we're, um...such huge music fans!" yelled Bon Bon.

Lyra spun around in time with Bon Bon. "Uh...yeah! We really want to meet Sapphire Shores!" Lyra added. "And to dance with you!" Soon, the three ponies were moving in sync, looking almost like a choreographed trio.

The crowd that had gathered was watching the trio. "What an interesting routine," said Lyrica Lilac, eyes alight with something halfway between wonder and confusion. "It's so intriguing yet so...*silly*?"

"Well, it's definitely the best attempt I've seen to get this shindig started," Sapphire Shores agreed, nodding along to the beat with

a huge smile on her face. "Even if it is a bit unconventional."

Pinkie skipped over to the wall, ran up it, and did a backflip off it. Lyra tried to copy her, but she just slid down the wall. Turning her mistake into a fluid interpretive move, she sprang up. Bon Bon flailed her hooves around to distract everypony while Lyra regained her composure.

"Songbird, look over there!" Songbird Serenade's assistant, Crownpiece, nudged her boss in Pinkie's direction. "She's much better than Countess Coloratura's dancers, don't you think?"

Songbird Serenade pushed her thick black-and-yellow bangs away from her face for a better look. As she watched Pinkie bounce up to the ballroom ceiling, defying all gravity, Songbird gasped in wonder. "Is she... is she... *swinging* from the chandelier?"

"Whoa," Crownpiece marveled. Her blue eyes were bright with astonishment. "That was unreal!"

Pinkie Pie twirled toward her party cannon, which Cheese had just rolled out. She stepped back, took a running leap, then jumped onto the cannon and pulled the lever! Thousands of glittering confetti stars burst forth and rained down onto the partygoers. Everypony cheered and rushed the dance floor. Pinkie felt her heart beating in time to the music. She'd done it! With their huge smiles and silly dance moves, the star attendees seemed to be shining brighter than they ever had before, launching the Pony Popstravaganza into the stratosphere as a sparkling success.

But there was one important pony who was still unsatisfied.

CHAPTER FOUR

For the rest of the evening, Songbird Serenade wasn't able to keep her mind off the amazing impromptu dance display. She'd never seen anypony who had such unique moves in her whole career. The pink pony had been filled with an enthusiasm and joy that was uplifting, yet she had such weird moves. It was exactly the vibe Songbird Serenade had been searching for to spice up her own act.

When Songbird saw something she liked, she didn't waste any time.

"Crownpiece! I need you!" Songbird called out, trotting over to the Unicorn mare with the wavy golden mane and crown-shaped cutie mark. "You *have* to find her." Songbird's black-and-yellow fringe hung down over her eyes again. Sometimes this made it really difficult to tell if the singer was joking or being serious.

"Find who?" Crownpiece said through the last bite of her slice of starfruit tart. She wiped her mouth with her hoof and pushed her gold mane out of her face. Then Crownpiece pulled out the huge purple notepad she brought everywhere in case she needed to write anything down for Songbird Serenade—rehearsals, costume fittings, and other appointments. She flipped past a page with the set designs of giant gilded birdcages for Songbird's lavish aviary-themed Glammy performance piece, and found a blank one.

"That plucky pink pony you pointed out!" Songbird urged under her breath. She craned her neck around. "I need to speak with her right away. I've been struck by a brilliant idea for my Glammy performance," Songbird trilled. "Hurry! This party is almost over, and I'm going to miss my chance!"

Crownpiece's mind began to race, imagining the extra work she would have to put in thanks to this brilliant new idea, but she nodded obediently and trotted off into the ballroom to appease her boss. The request did strike her as odd, however. Songbird Serenade was not usually a demanding diva like other pop stars she had heard about, such as Countess Coloratura. Crownpiece had

heard some nightmare stories about Rara and her constant demands, even though she'd supposedly changed her ways by now. Crownpiece personally thought Rara's reformation and new-found sincerity seemed a bit phony and were just more parts of her ostentatious act.

Lots of pop stars were like that, thought Crownpiece. She passed by Sapphire Shores regaling a group of yes-ponies with a story about her latest dolphin dream, and Jewel Tone calling her makeup mare over to re-powder her muzzle. It was all a part of the show.

Crownpiece pushed her way around the crowded dance floor three times without any sightings of the mare in question. She slumped in defeat. Where was that elusive pink dancing pony? Crownpiece really didn't want to go back and tell Songbird she'd failed at such a simple request. It was really important that she stick with this job, at least until the Glammy Awards night. Then she could do whatever she wanted.

Suddenly, a glamorous Unicorn with a purple mane and an over-the-top blue-and-teal organza gown caught Crownpiece's eye. From the way she was waving hello to everypony, Crownpiece got the sense that she knew what was going on. "Excuse me, Miss—um—Miss—?" Crownpiece stammered over the music.

"Please, call me *Rarity*!" she said as she spun around, beaming with delight. Rarity extended her polished hoof. "Fashion designer to the stars *and* the common pony with taste. Pleased to make your acquaintance, Crownpiece."

Crownpiece blushed. "You know who I am?"

"Oh, of course, darling." Rarity laughed. "You're Songbird Serenade's new assistant. I just saw a photo of you standing by her in *PegasUS Weekly*." Rarity leaned in and whispered under her breath so as not to appear gauche. "So exciting! That's the job hundreds of mares would absolutely live for."

"I know!" Crownpiece nodded and her pretty golden mane caught the light. "As soon as I met her, I practically begged her for the job. Plus, I get to come to parties like this!" Crownpiece motioned to the decorated ballroom. Things were finally beginning to wind down.

"Please tell me Songbird enjoyed herself tonight? My friend Pinkie Pie planned this soiree and I think she was quite nervous that nopony liked it at first—"

"Pinkie Pie?" Crownpiece's eyes lit up. "Is she

the one with the curly mane and all the confetti cannons? And that totally wild dancing?"

"Yes, yes. That's her." Rarity let out a tiny chuckle and shook her head. "Oh dear, she does get a tad carried away, but I assure you she *is* lovely—"

"Help me!" Crownpiece blurted out in desperation.

"Help you?" Rarity's face fell. "Are you all right, darling?"

"Sorry." Crownpiece blushed with embarrassment as she pulled out her notepad. "What I *meant* to say was that Songbird Serenade would like to talk to your friend Pinkie Pie. Um...uh...can you arrange a meeting?"

"A meeting with *Songbird Serenade*?" Rarity's eyes grew wide with delight. "Consider it done. Have Songbird meet me by the starfish tank in two minutes!" she yelled out as she disappeared with an excited canter into the crowd.

Crownpiece grinned at her minor victory. Maybe she was finally getting the hang of this assistant thing, after all.

CHAPTER FIVE

Whoa. Are you *serious*?!" squeaked Pinkie
Pie, mouth agape. She had just changed
out of her foam star costume and was now
wearing a giant crescent moon on her head.
She'd been heading outside with Cheese to get
in place for the big party-ending sparkler send-
off when Rarity had snatched her and dragged
her back inside.

Now Pinkie Pie was facing a famous pop star who had asked specifically for her. Pinkie shook her moon head in disbelief. "You—Songbird Serenade—want *me*—a totally average, not-professional-dancer party pony—to perform with *you*, the biggest pop star in Equestria since Countess Coloratura, in the Glammy performance that could win you the most prestigious honor of your entire career?!"

"That's right! I don't just want you in my act—I *need* you in my act! You're going to save everypony in the audience from boredom." Songbird Serenade nodded with a coy smirk. "See that?" Songbird made a face and motioned across the room to where the colt wonder Feather Bangs was trying to impress Ritzy Rose and Moonlight Melody by bragging about his new album. Their conversation looked rehearsed.

"I bet they're having the same conversation they just had with ten other ponies. Every year, the Glammys are the same—the same old ponies, the same parties, and the same boring over-the-top performances. If I'm going to be a part of it, I refuse to maintain the status quo!" Songbird Serenade shook her head. Her thick bangs remained covering her eyes, but Pinkie could tell that she was excited. "I want to push the envelope! I want to stand out...by stepping out of the spotlight and putting you in it." Songbird seemed proud of herself, but Pinkie was a tad confused. "So...what do you say? Do you want to be my star?"

"Well..." Pinkie Pie bit her lip. She'd never

done anything like a Glammy performance before, but that didn't mean she couldn't try. Still, Pinkie couldn't help feeling that it might be a lot of pressure! What if she messed up and then Songbird lost the award? That would make Pinkie Pie feel ickier than a burned sticky bun.

Crownpiece shuffled anxiously. Part of her wished that Pinkie would say no so she wouldn't have to redo her work and change any of the details for Songbird's performance. The Glammy Awards were only a week away, and there were still so many things to iron out. Adding a new design element, or a new pony performer, to the act would complicate everything.

But Pinkie Pie just stood there with a funny expression on her face.

"Songbird," Rarity interjected with a pleading smile. It was embarrassing that her friend was taking so long to respond to a question whose correct answer was clearly quite obvious. "Would you excuse us for a moment? Pinkie and I need to have a quick word...."

"Take your time." Songbird nodded as Rarity yanked her friend out of earshot.

"Pinkamena Diane Pie—what in Equestria are you doing? You simply have to say yes!" Rarity stomped her hoof on the ground like a filly and looked around to make sure nopony was listening. Then her words came tumbling out like a kicked barrel of apples. "This is an amazing opportunity! Think of all the ponies you could make smile with your dance. Besides, Songbird Serenade is one of the only Glammy nominees who I've yet to design a look for. If you help her out...perhaps she'll be open to hearing my ideas for her spring tour!"

Rarity squealed, and gave Pinkie Pie a little nudge. "Also, did I mention Glammy Week is full of parties?"

"Parties and helping out my bestie? Why didn't you just say so?" Pinkie giggled. "Sign me up!"

"Really?" Rarity's eyes sparkled with delight. "Oh, Pinkie, thank you ever so much! You really are sweeter than one of your strawberry short-cupcakes. I do owe you—"

"All right, all right…" Pinkie adjusted her moon headpiece and raised her eyebrows with a cheesy smirk. "Now quit *mooning* about it!" But as Rarity cantered off to deliver the good news, Pinkie Pie felt a funny feeling rising in her tummy. Were those nervicitement butterflies? Exactly what had Pinkie gotten herself into this time?

CHAPTER SIX

Crownpiece had told Pinkie to be at the Stables Center at eight o'clock sharp. It was going to be a long day for everypony, but even longer for Pinkie Pie, since she had no idea what she was doing.

After she'd arrived, Pinkie Pie still had no clue what to do. She plopped herself down in the audience of the massive theater, with those butterflies still flitting about in her tummy. As she waited for Crownpiece and watched all the pop star ponies getting ready for their first day of rehearsals and sound checks onstage, Pinkie felt as if her butterflies were multiplying like parasprites! She didn't belong here with these fancy, famous fillies. Pinkie Pie wasn't a star! She was just a simple party pony from Ponyville. She was about to stand up and leave, when a familiar voice startled her.

"Morning, Pinkie Pie! Sorry I'm so late!" Crownpiece called out, causing Pinkie Pie to jump up from her seat in surprise. "We had a crisis with the seamstress. Poor thing stayed up all night sewing the costumes for Songbird's new and improved idea."

This was Pinkie's chance! "If you need somepony who knows fashion stuff, I have just

the gal. Rarity—the best in the business. She would love to help!"

"Oh really? Rarity? I met her at the Pop-stravaganza! I'll tell Songbird about her generous offer."

Crownpiece took a sip from her apple juice and wiped the sweat away from her forehead. "Anyway, I'm so happy you made it! You can just stay put for now, then we'll get you onstage to perform the choreography, okay? I told your other dancers to be here in twenty."

"Other dancers?" Pinkie said, puzzled. "But I don't have any other—"

"Oh no!" Crownpiece's face fell. "*Please* don't tell me I invited two random clingers to this exclusive rehearsal." She put her hoof to her head in agony. "I'll be in so much trouble with Jazz Hoof. I've been warned that he hates it

when anypony sees his work before it's ready." Crownpiece riffled through her note files and read from a piece of parchment. "So you don't know Lyra Heartstrings and Bon Bon? They insisted they were with you!"

Instantly, Pinkie Pie flashed back to the past couple of days. Lyra and Bon Bon had been at Hay's Pizza, and then they'd joined her on the dance floor at the party. What exactly did those sneaky ponies want? Pinkie's Pinkie Sense was tingling. Something was fishy here, and it wasn't the tuna sandwich she'd brought for lunch.

"Oh, silly me!" Pinkie Pie said to cover. "Lyra and Bon Bon are totally my other dancers. Yup, yup."

"Thank Celestia." Crownpiece wiped the sweat from her brow again and sighed with

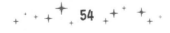

relief. Then she began to recheck her schedules. A few papers fell out and floated to the floor. Pinkie snatched them up and passed them back to her. "Oh, thank you! I really have to fix that folder. It keeps doing that." Crownpiece blushed as she shoved them back in with the others. "Okay, gotta run. So much to do! You can watch from here until Songbird calls you up."

All eight nominees for Pop Pony of the Year stood onstage, dressed in their finest rehearsal clothes. Based on the exhaustive Glammy Week schedule Crownpiece had given Pinkie Pie, she was supposed to be around for all this stuff. But it was already so boring. There hadn't been any more parties or even an invite. Unless Pinkie Pie counted the waffle party she'd thrown for herself and Gummy Snap, her pet alligator, that morning at breakfast.

Everypony seemed super tired. Ritzy Rose and Moonlight Melody stifled yawns and tried to stretch themselves awake. They were clearly not morning ponies. They took turns sipping from a carafe of mint tea and complaining about the bags underneath their eyes. Pinkie Pie wondered if those two were always grumpy. It sure seemed like it!

"Welcome, nominees!" barked Jazz Hoof, the show's resident host and director. He trotted in wearing a purple jumpsuit and a rainbow sweatband around his spiky yellow mane. "Obviously, you're all incredibly talented musicians, which is why you're here today." As he spoke, Jazz Hoof marched back and forth across the stage like a cross between the captain of the Royal Guard and a supermodel. "First and foremost, the Glammy Awards are all about *you*, you gorgeous creatures! Congrats, everypony."

Daisy Chain exchanged an excited look with Feather Bangs. It was the first year either of them had been nominated—Daisy Chain for her sweet country tunes, and Feather Bangs for his cheesy crooning. Feather winked at Daisy and she burst into a fit of giggles. Countess Coloratura and Jewel Tone rolled their eyes. That young stallion had no shame.

"It's true that everypony on this stage is nominated for Pop Pony of the Year..." Jazz Hoof said with a dramatic flip of his mane. He closed his eyes and turned his muzzle up to the ceiling of the theater as if he were mustering the strength to deliver the rest of his sentence. The sparkly eye shadow he was wearing for dramatic effect caught the light. "But only

one of you will take home the honor. So it goes without saying that these performances must be *everything*." Jazz Hoof raised a perfectly plucked eyebrow. "If you want to win, that is."

A murmur of excited whispers erupted among the nominees.

"*Wooooo!*" Pinkie cheered into her megaphone. "Go, *Songbiiiiiird*! You can do it!" She had wanted to throw some confetti, but she was all out. Pinkie had just begun to look through her bag for some streamers or a supportive sign to hold up, when Jazz Hoof called out from the stage.

"Who's out there?" he shouted, annoyed.

"It's *meeeee!*" Pinkie Pie called out. "Don't worry; I think I have an extra rubber chicken in here if it encourages you. Chickens are birds, so that works?" Pinkie shrugged, and waved the chicken in the air like a pennant flag. "Go, Song Chicken! Whoopsies! I mean... *GO, SONGBIRD!*"

"'Song chicken'? What in the glittery go-go boots is that pony on about?" Jazz Hoof muttered to the musicians. "Don't worry, I'll take care of this." He rolled his eyes and turned back to the seats. "This is a closed rehearsal! Please leave at once, whoever you are, or we'll have you escorted out by security!"

That pony was so rude that it made Pinkie Pie want to storm out, but instead she decided that maybe she could teach Jazz Hoof and these pop ponies a thing or two about friendship.

Pinkie Pie was here to stay, whether they liked it or not.

CHAPTER SEVEN

It's my new friend Pinkie Pie. She's with me!" Songbird chirped. Everypony strained to look at the offender, shielding their eyes with their hooves so they could catch a glimpse of her in the darkened seats.

"Well, that's nice, Songbird." Jazz Hoof sighed. "But what is she doing here? Glammy rehearsals are only for singers and dancers."

"Oh! Sorry if this throws anypony off, but I've decided to change my performance." Songbird Serenade took a step forward and turned to her fellow nominees. "Instead of a big show with crazy costumes and sets, there's just going to be me, and a spotlight on Pinkie Pie...*dressed as* me!" Songbird grinned and waved her hoof through the air to illustrate her point. "I really think that her dance moves will represent my words better than a flashy set can. It's going to be so unexpected and raw. I can't wait! What do you think?"

Nopony said anything, but the other nominees did seem to be feeling quite the range of emotions. Sapphire Shores looked taken aback, while Ritzy Rose and Moonlight Melody tried desperately to stifle their snickers. Feather Bangs, Daisy Chain, and Jewel Tone just seemed confused. Countess Coloratura was the only one who was nodding along in approval. "That actually sounds incredible! It kinda reminds me of the Helping Hooves Music Festival performance I did in Ponyville. Can I—?"

"No, no, no!" Jazz Hoof interrupted as he trotted over to Songbird Serenade. "This just won't do. Nopony is allowed to make any changes to anything. Doesn't anypony remember this year's theme?" More than anything in life, Jazz Hoof loved a solid theme.

"It's 'Musical Menagerie'!" Daisy Chain interjected with a chirpy tone. Her curly yellow mane bounced as she nodded enthusiastically. "Our acts are all supposed to be inspired by different animals! Mine features cows, Sapphire's has a dolphin theme, Feather's is—"

"That's right, Daisy," Jazz Hoof interrupted again. "It's brilliant. And I worked hard to arrange everything that you all preordered. Songbird—what about your aviary-themed sets? Those giant gold birdcages were going to be everything! *Everything.*" Jazz Hoof let out a big sigh and put his hoof to his forehead. "If you don't use them, then I just can't even."

"You can't even what?" asked Pinkie Pie, finally trotting up the stairs to join the nominees on the stage.

"You know... *I can't even!*" Jazz Hoof was getting impatient. So were the other pop stars, who all began calling their assistants over to not-so-subtly whisper orders into their ears.

"*Ooh! Ooh!* Let me guess!" Pinkie rubbed her chin thoughtfully. "You can't even... find your favorite rubber ducky and now you're really sad because bath time is way less fun? Or maybe you can't even decide what flavor of ice cream to eat for dinner...?" Pinkie Pie slumped. "Wow, that would be really sad, actually. If you need any ice cream guidance, I'm here, buddy."

Jazz Hoof turned to Songbird and raised his sparkly eyebrows at her. He was clearly not impressed with this turn of events.

"Trust me, Jazz." Songbird Serenade shrugged with a smirk. "We don't need big, fancy sets— Pinkie Pie is going to steal the show!"

"She'd better," muttered Ritzy Rose to Moonlight Melody, loud enough for Pinkie Pie to hear. "Or Songbird Serenade might have just lost herself Pop Pony of the Year." Moonlight and Ritzy hoof-bumped. With their biggest competition—Songbird Serenade—out, they'd be one step closer to winning.

It was all Pinkie Pie needed to hear. No way

was she going to let a bunch of meanies win that award over her kind new friend! Pinkie Pie puffed out her chest and made a Pinkie Promise to herself.

She would dance like nopony was watching.

CHAPTER EIGHT

A heavy beat boomed through the Stables Center, echoing through the cavernous space as Sapphire Shores bounced around the stage, joined by twelve ponies wearing dolphin-print dresses. Waves constructed out of huge wood panels painted blue swayed back and forth in front of them. *"Feel the waves! Let the rhythm wash over you! Wave your hooves to the motion...*

motion of the ocean!" Sapphire Shores belted out. Even though it was only the first dress rehearsal for the Pop Pony of the Year nominees, everypony looked and sounded flawless.

Backstage, everypony else was preparing for their turns on the stage. Songbird Serenade's new song, "Crystal Heart," was up next on the schedule. She quietly sang the lyrics to herself, stomping her hoof to keep time. *"Whoaaaa, I've got strong hooves and a crystal heart ... but your magic spells might be too smart!"*

A sound assistant pony came up and passed Songbird a headset microphone. "Your assistant told me you preferred headset sound to Unicorn magic amplifiers, is that right?"

"That's right." Songbird winked at him and held up the microphone. "Once again, Crownpiece has thought of everything." The singer trotted over to Pinkie Pie, who was busy doing stretches in front of a standing mirror. Pinkie Pie seemed tense.

"Songbird...are you sure I'm ready for this?! I really want to do the best job dancing ever," Pinkie Pie confessed. The only preparation Pinkie Pie had done so far was getting fitted for a mane wig that matched Songbird's signature style—yellow on one side and black on the other, with choppy bangs hanging down over her eyes. The huge pink bow on the back of her head and black high-necked top just like Songbird's really brought the look together.

"Of course I'm sure, Pinkie!" Songbird Serenade assured. "Plus, you *all* look perfect. I just love these costumes. So much better than the feathered, light-up leotards you were supposed to be wearing. Simplicity is so underrated, don't you think?"

"Yeah!" Lyra and Bon Bon replied in unison, nodding. Their costumes were just plain black dresses with no frills or feathers whatsoever. Pinkie Pie still hadn't been able to figure out why Lyra and Bon Bon were here. She was going to ask them, but as soon as the duo had arrived, they'd excused themselves for a "tour" of the theater. When they'd returned hours later, they were both wearing black sunglasses and looked stressed out. Then Songbird had brought them up to the stage. Very suspicious.

"Sorry we took so long in our…uh…*costume fitting* earlier!" Lyra said apologetically. She tugged at her black dress.

"Did we miss anything?" Bon Bon said, her voice wavering with nerves. "What are we even supposed to be doing out there?"

"Relax, girls," Songbird insisted. "Just do

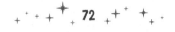

exactly what you did at the party and I'll take care of the rest. We're going to be magnificent! And if we're not, it doesn't matter, because nopony is in the audience today. That's why it's called a rehearsal!" Songbird chuckled and walked off to do some more vocal exercises. She was always so coolheaded and professional. It was no wonder the other pop stars were so intimidated by her.

While Songbird was out of earshot, Pinkie Pie took her chance to dig for details. "All right, you two. My Pinkie Sense has been tingling since the moment you took your first bite of a cheesy slice at Hay's Pizza. Why were you there? And then at the party?" Pinkie Pie narrowed her eyes, even though Lyra and Bon Bon couldn't see this through her thick Songbird wig. "You've been slinking around me like two sneaky snakes for days! I'm onto you...."

Lyra's and Bon Bon's faces fell. They quickly exchanged a guilty look—the look of two ponies who had been caught. A moment of silence passed as they considered their next move.

"Aha!" Pinkie Pie pointed her hoof at Bon Bon, triumphant. "I was right! You *are* up to something."

Finally, Bon Bon spoke. "All right, fine. You caught us. What do you know?"

Onstage, Sapphire Shores and her team were still practicing. They were on the sixth run-through of their number. Sapphire was attempting to rework the choreography, due to somepony tripping over the wooden waves in the final verse and nearly knocking the star off the stage in the process. Jazz Hoof was flitting about, giving orders and opinions to Sapphire Shores like a hyper hummingbird with a belly full of nectar.

"Sugarcane!" he barked before taking a sip of his gigantic iced green tea. "When I said stay in line, I *meant* it. Okay, ladies, get in formation!" Sugarcane nodded and scrambled back to her spot and the music began again.

Sapphire counted them in. "And five . . . six . . . five, six, seven, eight . . . *BA-BAM!*"

"So what is it, girls?" Pinkie Pie pried, bringing the attention back to the matter at hoof. She walked in a circle around them to intimidate them, just like Shadow Spade did to the suspects in her best-selling mystery novels. "Planning a little heist, are we? Stealing somepony's identity, *hmmm*? Trying to get closer to the biggest pop star in Equestria so you can ponynap her and demand a ransom of a

thousand chocolate chip cookies?!" Pinkie Pie leaned in so close they could smell the cupcakes on her breath. "Which is it?"

"Pinkie Pie, what we are about to tell you may shock you…" Lyra explained, lowering her voice to a whisper even though the music was loud enough to mask their conversation. "But it won't be the first time you've heard it. Last time, things got too out of hoof and we had to do a Reflection Deflection spell on you and—"

"No *way*!" Pinkie Pie scoffed, causing Songbird to stop singing and look over. Pinkie Pie smiled and waved at her. When Songbird waved back, Pinkie turned back to Lyra and Bon Bon. She pushed up her wig's bangs so the ponies would know she meant business. "If somepony had performed a spell on me, I would definitely remember it happening!" Pinkie Pie had an incredibly accurate memory for details. It's how she knew everypony in Ponyville's birthday, favorite flavor of cake, and favorite balloon colors.

"Normally, yes. But not if it's a *memory-erasing* spell..." Bon Bon said through gritted teeth. "But look, that's not the point."

"Exactly!" Pinkie Pie nodded, triumphant. "The point is..." She scratched her wig-head. "Wait—what was the point again?" Maybe the memory-erasing spell had erased more than she thought.

"The point is, you asked what we are doing here." Bon Bon's face grew serious. "Lyra and I are here on a mission to—"

But before the pony could finish her sentence, a bloodcurdling shriek rang out from behind one of the backstage curtains.

CHAPTER NINE

Ritzy Rose pushed the heavy velvet curtains aside and tore past Pinkie Pie.

"AHHHHHH! MY SETS!" She burst out onto the stage, causing Sapphire Shores and her dancers' routine to come to a screeching halt. The music stopped as Ritzy Rose cried out again. Her pretty face contorted into an expression of despair. "All my beautiful sets have been ruined!"

"Who would do such a thing?" Moonlight Melody asked as she rushed out to the stage to support her friend. She put a supportive hoof on Ritzy's back. "Are you sure?"

"Yes, I'm sure. Somepony is clearly trying to sabotage me!" whined Ritzy Rose, jutting out her red-painted lips. "Of course this would happen to *me*!"

"Everypony, take five while we check this out." Jazz Hoof sighed, and waved his hoof at Sapphire Shores and her dancers. They scattered into groups to whisper about the drama. Jazz Hoof seemed skeptical of the claim, and for good reason. Ritzy Rose was known in the music community as the pony most likely to make a mountain out of a Breezie hill. Last year, the Pegasus had made a huge fuss about the fact that there were red apples instead of green ones in her dressing room.

Even though Pinkie Pie really wanted to finish her conversation with Lyra and Bon Bon, she couldn't help following the curious group of ponies as Ritzy led the way to the storage area, where all the sets were being held. It was supposed to be locked up tight, but the heavy wooden door was wide open, with the gigantic metal padlock swinging.

The room had been cordoned off into eight sections—one for each of the Pop Pony of the Year nominees to store the over-the-top Musical Menagerie set pieces that Jazz Hoof had demanded they all order. There was so much wild and crazy stuff it reminded Pinkie Pie of her own party-supply cave back home in Ponyville.

"It's so beautiful...." Pinkie cooed as she trotted past a pair of giant sculpted swans that had slides built in to their backs for Moonlight

Melody's performance, a light-up Ursa Major backdrop for Jewel Tone's, and hundreds of stuffed bunnies for Feather Bangs's ridiculous number. There was even something that resembled Pinkie's giant party cannon! Only this one was black and painted with a big pink bow on the side.

"Over there!" Ritzy cried out dramatically. "See for yourselves!" Sure enough, Ritzy's section was a disaster. The teal and purple rhinestone platforms that her dancers were supposed to stand on during the show looked as if somepony had bucked holes into them, and the peacock-feather curtains had been ripped to shreds. Glittering feathery debris lay everywhere.

Everypony erupted into a tizzy. Jazz Hoof began pacing back and forth, tugging on his yellow mane and hyperventilating.

"Look!" wailed Daisy Chain. "Something's wrong with mine, too!" She galloped over to her section. All it had was a papier-mâché cow on wheels, a gingham curtain, and a bunch of hay bales made from glow sticks tied together. Daisy was obviously going for a country-glam look in her number. "Somepony moved my cow!"

"I think what you meant to say is that some-pony *moooooooooved* it," Pinkie corrected.

Everypony turned as Crownpiece burst into the storage room. She galloped over to Pinkie Pie and Songbird, nearly dropping her sad-dlebag full of notes and schedules in the pro-cess. "What happened? I came back from my errands and nopony was onstage!" Several other nominees were now discovering that their sets had also been tampered with, but none to the extent of Ritzy Rose's disaster. There was also iridescent rainbow glitter everywhere for some odd reason. Crownpiece paused and looked around at the sparkly destruction. "Did, uh...something happen?"

"I'm afraid so...." Songbird shook her head sadly. "It looks like poor Ritzy's sets have been ransacked."

"How terrible!" muttered Crownpiece. She hung her head, looking as if she might cry. Her wavy gold mane fell over her eyes. Then she quickly began fumbling with her files to look for something. "Maybe Ritzy Rose can go minimal with her performance like you?"

"Hey, that's weird! The culprit left your stuff alone, Rara." Pinkie Pie motioned to Countess Coloratura's storage area. The giant model of a tiger's head was completely intact. Perhaps whoever had committed the act had run out of time? "Maybe they just really like tigers."

Moonlight Melody appeared beside them. "That is really strange, now that you mention it. . . ." She raised a suspicious brow.

Immediately, Ritzy Rose's eyes moved right to Countess Coloratura. "Why would *your* things be the only ones untouched, Rara? Unless you had something to do with this..." Ritzy's piercing blue eyes bore into her.

Countess Coloratura opened her mouth, but all that came out were a few panicky stutters. "B–b–b–but I w–would never—"

It appeared that Rara was now the pony in the spotlight, but for all the wrong reasons.

CHAPTER TEN

"All right, everypony! Let's just cool our cutie marks for a second here!" Jazz Hoof interjected. The director galloped over before anypony else could make another baseless accusation. "Do *not* point hooves. Pop Pony of the Year is a competitive category, but none of us here would ever stoop so low as to ruin another's performance, right? That's amateur stuff! We are professionals."

Rara sighed with relief.

"Couldn't have said it better myself," replied Songbird Serenade. The two newbies, Daisy Chain and Feather Bangs, nodded in agreement, clearly hoping to appear above "amateur stuff." The others looked less convinced. Pinkie Pie couldn't help noticing that Moonlight and Ritzy seemed disappointed.

"Thank Celestia, we have enough time to fix these sets." Jazz Hoof trotted over to the door, leaned down, and inspected the broken door lock. It didn't look like the work of Unicorn magic. From the scratchy scrapes on the metal, it appeared as if somepony had picked it with a rusty tool. "But we obviously need to ramp up security around here because this isn't going to—"

"Cut the mustard?" Pinkie Pie finished for him. "Toot the flugelhorn? Burp the baby?"

"All of the above," Jazz Hoof replied sincerely. He faced the group and crossed his hooves. He was maintaining quite a cool composure compared to how he'd been when somepony had messed up a dance move. "Now, call in your best security ponies and designers, put yourselves back together, and get your flanks dancing again. The show must go on!" He stuck his muzzle up in the air and pranced out of the storage room to find himself a restorative cold-pressed fruit smoothie. Even for him, it appeared, this was too much drama. And he loved drama.

CHAPTER ELEVEN

Later that night, when Jazz Hoof had finally called "wrap" on the day, Pinkie Pie was pooped. She had never danced so much in her entire life! The pink pony had twirled, bounced, and four-stepped alongside Lyra and Bon Bon to Songbird's "Crystal Heart" about a billion times. And they had to get up tomorrow and do it all again. How did Songbird and other pop stars manage such a wacky schedule all year long?

Pinkie was already itching to plan a relaxation party at the swimming hole with her friends back in Ponyville when this was all over. Rainbow Dash would bring the floaties, Applejack would bring her cooler full of cold apple cider, Flutter-shy could make a picnic, Rarity would provide some pretty umbrellas, and Twilight would read them a story while they relaxed.

As Pinkie Pie trotted down from the stage and gathered her belongings, she kept her eye on Lyra and Bon Bon doing the same. They'd never finished telling Pinkie why they'd been following her! Pinkie waved to them.

But the pair was too busy whispering to each other to notice her flailing hoof motions. *"Psst!"* Pinkie Pie hissed, tossing a glittery party streamer toward them in a feeble attempt to get their attention. It arched over the sea of seats and landed perfectly, draped across Lyra's horn. They spun around in surprise.

"Whoopsies! Sorry, Lyra." Pinkie Pie grinned. "Didn't mean to startle you. Perhaps I *interrupted something?*"

"No, no." Lyra shook her head. "Of course not! We were just discussing what to, um... have for dinner." Her darting eyes said otherwise. Ever since the incident with the ruined sets earlier, Pinkie's suspicions had doubled: Lyra and Bon Bon were the only ponies who had been missing right before the act.

"Great!" Pinkie Pie replied, heading over. She put a hoof around each of them and grinned as she led them out of the Stables Center. "What are we having? I'm starving!"

The Manehattan night was warm. The sun was setting over the city, and ponies were rushing home from their office jobs. The streets were alive with excitement, and Pinkie's heartbeat matched it. She was going to confront Lyra and Bon Bon!

They'd only trotted about a block when Lyra pointed to a diner with a neon sign of a knife and fork. "This place looks good, right?" Pinkie Pie recognized the restaurant. She'd eaten here back when Rarity was having her boutique opening. Her tummy rumbled in anticipation as she remembered the many stacks of delicious waffles slathered in syrup that she'd consumed that day.

The ponies slid into a booth and placed their

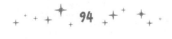

orders for three hayburgers, fries, and chocolate milk shakes with sprinkles on top.

"Tell me, gals," Pinkie Pie said through
slurps of milk shake. "Why did you ruin Ritzy
Rose's sets and why did you frame Countess
Coloratura for it?!"

"I was just about to ask the same thing,"
somepony interrupted.

Lyra, Bon Bon, and Pinkie Pie looked up to
see that Crownpiece was standing over their
table, looking very annoyed. "I stayed down
to inspect the storage room after everypony
went back upstairs and I found *these*." Crownpiece tossed a hoof-ful of peacock feathers from
Ritzy Rose's sets onto the table.

Bon Bon shrugged. "Some peacock feathers?"

"What does that prove?" asked Lyra through
a mouthful of fries.

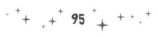

"Whoa." Pinkie Pie's eyes were as large as the plates on the table. "Are you guys actually birds? How have you been hiding this for so long? What's it like to be a bird? Have you spoken to Fluttershy about this?!"

Crownpiece rolled her eyes. "You two were missing for hours, and then I find this evidence. *You* were the ponies who sabotaged everything!" She plucked a feather from the table and held it up to Lyra's and Bon Bon's faces. Pinkie Pie could now see that there were several mint-green tail hairs tangled in it.

They were undeniably from Lyra. Immediately, she went stiff and exchanged a funny look with Bon Bon. "You've got it all wrong. We are just here to support Songbird Serenade."

"Not anymore, thanks to Pinkie Pie here spilling her suspicions earlier." Crownpiece sighed with visible regret. "Lyra, Bon Bon...I'm really sorry about this, but I've already alerted Jazz Hoof and security that I've found the ponies responsible. You two won't be allowed near the theater anymore." Crownpiece turned on her hoof and looked back over her shoulder.

"I've worked too hard on this production to let anypony's performance be ruined!" Then Crownpiece scurried off in a flash of silver and gold. Her mane billowed out behind her, leaving a cloud of glitter and scraps of paper from her files in her wake.

Pinkie Pie's jaw was already practically in her hayburger from the shock of it all when Bon Bon blurted out, "Pinkie Pie—we're secret agents!"

Lyra casually took a sip of her chocolate milk shake and then dropped the bomb. "We *were*

on an undercover mission to save the Glammy Awards from monstrous doom." She paused as Bon Bon pulled an envelope from her saddlebag and pushed it across the table. "But since our cover has been blown, now it looks as if you're going to have to take over the investigation by yourself.

"Pinkie Pie, if you don't find what we were looking for before the Glammy Awards, everypony will be in grave danger."

CHAPTER TWELVE

With all the information from Lyra and Bon Bon rattling around in Pinkie Pie's head like sprinkles in a can, she hightailed it to her hotel. Crownpiece already mistrusted Lyra and Bon Bon, and she seemed positive that they'd been at fault. But if Pinkie Pie could get Songbird to consider the other explanation, she could save the Glammy Awards from something bad. Something really, really bad! She had to find Songbird and talk to her— alone. She didn't want to freak out any more ponies than she needed to. Songbird was the perfect one to keep a cool head in the face of impending disaster.

The pink pony bounced through the city streets, but her little hooves weren't moving fast enough. Pinkie Pie pulled out her party whistle, which was pitched perfectly to be the most pleasant piercing noise on the planet. *FWEEEE!* It rang out into the street, and immediately a taxicab pulled up.

"Where to, miss?" said the bearded driver. He adjusted his newscolt cap and tipped it to her. "I'm heading uptown."

"Perfect! Me too." Pinkie Pie hopped in. "The Foal Seasons, please! And I'm in a hurry."

"Everypony always is!"

Moments later, the taxicab came to a screeching halt. Pinkie tossed the driver some bits and thanked him. She made her way upstairs, trying to remember exactly which room belonged to Songbird Serenade. But Pinkie Pie didn't need to search long, because two burly security guard Unicorns were stationed outside of it. Vinny had a long brown mane tied back and Whinnyfield had a short, curly dark mane. They both wore black suits and sunglasses. Pinkie Pie wondered if they were part of Lyra and Bon Bon's secret agency, too.

"Step aside, gentlecolts! I'm here to speak with Songbird Serenade!" Pinkie Pie declared with a bow. She thought the extra flourish might show them how serious she was. But the stallions didn't move. "Look, fellas. She knows

me. The name's Pinkie Pie? I'm her dancer? Oh, come on!"

The Unicorn with the curly mane just grunted in response.

"Pinkie!" Songbird flung open the door and pulled Pinkie Pie into the room. The luxurious suite was made up of several rooms decked out in lush fabrics of teal and red. A giant bouquet of flowers sat on the counter along with a range of various fruit baskets. Rarity would have been in heaven.

"I'm so sorry about that. Jazz Hoof demanded we all bring in our extra security and everything after the incident today...." Songbird apologized as she led Pinkie over to the sofa. She began to pour two steaming mugs of hot cocoa. "I just feel so silly for accidentally causing all this extra drama with my last-minute whims and wild ideas! At least it's all settled now and we can move on with the show." She sighed with the weight of the world and took a sip of cocoa. "I still can't believe it was Lyra and Bon Bon all along! They seemed so lovely."

"But it wasn't them!" Pinkie blurted out, nearly spitting hot cocoa onto Songbird's face.

"Earlier, you said that they were the ones who ruined everything—"

"I know." Pinkie put down her mug and hung her head. Her fluffy fuchsia mane started to go a little flat. "But actually, that's why I'm here. I've made a huge mistake."

Songbird stood up, aghast. "What do you mean?" There was nothing worse than wrongly accusing somepony who was innocent.

"Well…" Pinkie Pie took a deep breath and

it all came tumbling out really fast. "See, Lyra and Bon Bon were acting super shady, and then they went missing right before all the sets were ruined, so I was sure they were trying to *ruin* the Glammys. . . ." Pinkie gave an embarrassed laugh. "But as it turns out, they were actually trying to *save* the Glammys, because they're undercover agents for the Secret Monster Intelligence League of Equestria! This really scary monster was in this box-thingy that the secret agents use to trap the monsters and send them to the big baddie-monster jail, Tartarus! But this one 'Pondora Box' was stolen from Lyra and Bon Bon while they were bringing it to the secret hidequarters, but the magic tracker on it said that it was at the Stables Center, so basically—"

"Somepony's plotting to ruin the Glammys

with a stolen monster"—Songbird Serenade spoke very slowly, as if she couldn't believe what was coming out of her own mouth— "trapped in a box?"

"Yep." Pinkie Pie shrugged. "Pretty much."

Songbird's mind began to race with horrific visions of big bugbears and massive Manticores barreling across the stage, wreaking havoc during Daisy Chain's sweet farm song and Sapphire Shore's sassy melody. Not exactly the show they wanted to put on. They had to stop it—whatever "it" was.

"Sweet Luna..." Songbird began to pace back and forth in the massive room. It was a lot to take in. "What are we going to do?"

"Figure out who stole the box." Pinkie Pie rubbed her hooves together. "And find it before it's too late! Are you with me?"

Songbird nodded without hesitation, even though she felt nervous. She was no secret agent. But Songbird couldn't just stand by and let anything happen. If she could save her colleagues and friends from a monster, there was no way she was going to stay in her comfort zone. "I'm with you."

And with that, the two ponies began to devise a plan.

CHAPTER THIRTEEN

Over the next few days, Pinkie Pie and Song-bird Serenade used every spare moment they had to search for clues that might lead them to information regarding the Pondora Box. They had little to go on except the fact that Lyra and Bon Bon were positive that it was somewhere in the Stables Center.

But as the Glammy Awards edged closer

day by day, Pinkie Pie and Songbird Serenade still had nothing. They'd searched every inch of the theater, trying to appear as inconspicuous as possible. Luckily, everypony else was so wrapped up in the coming show that they hardly noticed the duo slinking around. Or if they did, they probably thought it was some other new, weird part of Songbird's performance revamp.

In addition to the search, rehearsals had become even more intense. Each of the Pop Pony of the Year nominees (along with their entourages) were expected to put in extra hours of work. Along with all the last-minute choreography changes and costume fittings, there were also interviews with media outlets and magazines such as *PegasUS Weekly*, *Mare Éclair*, and *Ponies*. Everypony was overwhelmed.

When Jewel Tone requested an afternoon off to go swimming at the hotel pool, Jazz Hoof firmly denied her request. Everypony got the sense that Jazz Hoof was pushing them even harder than usual this year. Every day, he demanded more and more from the nominees, but nopony could figure out why. Every day, he ran around in his brightly colored jumpsuits, barking orders and being unsatisfied with most of what he saw.

One morning, Pinkie Pie was tying her bushy mane up into a bun in the dressing room when she overheard Ritzy Rose, Jewel Tone, and Moonlight Melody gossiping about him. They hadn't noticed Pinkie Pie, so she slunk into a rack of costumes to watch and listen.

"I think Jazz Hoof is losing his mind 'cause they're firing him after this year!" whispered

Jewel Tone. "He's trying to make a splash before he leaves. That's why everything has to be perfect."

"They *are*?" Moonlight Melody gasped, mid–lipstick application. "But he's been the face of the Glammys since I was a filly!"

"Apparently, Countess Coloratura said something to the producers last year about his ideas being old and unoriginal. Even though that isn't very nice, I sort of agree," added Ritzy Rose. "Don't you?"

"Oh yes." Jewel Tone nodded in agreement. She used her magic to pin a star-shaped clip into her shiny teal mane and inspected herself in the lighted mirror. "Jazz Hoof is old news. He forced that whole Musical Menagerie theme on us and now he's overdoing it again. No wonder I've never even come close to winning Pop

Pony of the Year! It's because my act is all over the place...."

"It's kind of crazy"—Moonlight gave a devious little chuckle—"that even though we don't like Rara, maybe she did us all a favor?"

Ritzy Rose lowered her voice and raised her eyebrows. A tiny smile danced on her painted lips. "At least now we're all thinking *out of the box* on that topic and we can guarantee that this year's awards show is going to be epic, no matter what." The three ponies cackled with laughter, even though it didn't sound like a joke to Pinkie Pie. Then they trotted out of the room together.

Out of the box! Something pinged in Pinkie Pie's head. Was it possible that Ritzy Rose could be referring to the stolen Pondora Box that Lyra and Bon Bon had been searching for?

Ritzy *did* seem to have a nasty attitude from the start. Maybe she was the pony who was bent on ruining the awards....

Pinkie Pie tore out of the dressing room to go find Songbird and report her most recent findings. But when Pinkie found her comrade, she was in deep conversation with Crownpiece. Pinkie Pie and Songbird had agreed not to reveal anything to the poor assistant because she was already so stressed out as it was.

The circles under Crownpiece's eyes were getting darker every day and her golden mane was looking frizzier by the minute. Plus, Pinkie Pie was super-duper grateful that Crownpiece had contacted Rarity to make a couture dress for Songbird to wear before the big night. Pinkie didn't want to risk overloading Crownpiece and messing that up.

"The gown should be delivered by tonight," Crownpiece explained, barely looking up from writing in her notebook. "Rarity followed your requests perfectly. Chic, simple, and understated, with a pop of pink." The assistant passed her boss a steaming cup of tea. "Drink this. Dandelion, good for your vocal cords."

"You're so organized, Crownpiece," Songbird praised, gratefully taking a sip of the hot beverage. "I heard you've even been helping out the Glammy organizers. Is there anything you can't do?"

"Honestly?" Crownpiece smirked. "No, probably not. If something is happening around here, you can bet I've had a hoof in it! Actually, that reminds me, I promised I'd help Jazz Hoof and the show producers with the ballot boxes."

"Ballot boxes?" Pinkie interrupted. "Is that where ponies vote for their favorite singers?"

"*Mmm-hmmm.*" Crownpiece nodded. "The way it works is that each box must be enchanted by a Unicorn to correctly count the votes and keep it a secret locked inside until the big night. It takes a really long time and they need all the Unicorn power they can get, so I've got to gallop!" And then Crownpiece was off again.

"Speaking of boxes"—Pinkie Pie leaned in to Songbird and whispered—"I think I have a hot tip in the investigation. . . ."

"Really?" Songbird pushed her bangs away from her face to survey potential eavesdroppers. Daisy Chain and Sapphire Shores were nearby, talking about how "it was an honor just to be *nominated* for a Glammy, let alone win one." A group of security ponies were helping themselves to coffee from the craft services table. And Feather Bangs was busy practicing his acceptance speech to himself, blowing the "crowd" fake kisses and winking.

It was too risky here.

"Come on!" Songbird began to trot through the halls to put some distance between them, and Pinkie followed dutifully. When they were finally in the hallway behind the dressing rooms, she asked, "Okay, what do you have?"

Pinkie Pie paused for dramatic effect. "Ritzy Rose! I heard her mention the phrase 'out of the box.' You know...like a monster...coming out of a box?"

Pinkie Pie pulled out the worn, folded piece of paper that had been given to her by Lyra and Bon Bon. On it was a drawing of a silver box engraved with intricate crosshatch

designs—the elusive Pondora Box. "Coincidence? I think not."

A few stagehooves trotted past, pushing a cart carrying Ritzy Rose's brand-new replacement sets. Pinkie and Songbird shot them smiles and waited till they were gone again.

"Ritzy Rose has been acting bitter ever since last year's show," Songbird recalled. "She thought for sure she was a horseshoe-in for at least one award. But then Countess Coloratura took home almost everything. She was pretty upset."

DING! A bell went off in Pinkie's head. She'd heard those ponies talking about Rara, too! Not to mention what they'd said about Jazz Hoof being fired from his job. Both ponies had reason to be mad at the Glammy Awards.

There had to be some connection among Ritzy, Rara, or Jazz Hoof in all this.

Pinkie Pie wished she and Songbird had more time to try to understand what exactly was going on, to plot out the dots and their relation to one another.

But the truth was, they only had one day left to make them connect.

CHAPTER FOURTEEN

I'm going to see what I can find hiding in Ritzy Rose's things with my little spy eyes," Pinkie Pie said as she took off toward the dressing room. Maybe the box has been there all along, right under their muzzles.

"And I'll keep mine on Jazz Hoof," Songbird Serenade mumbled to herself. Perhaps she could just talk to him and see what he knew.

Since she'd been nominated for the past few years, Songbird felt like she'd gotten to know the colorful Jazz Hoof pretty well. He loved the Glammy Awards with all his heart—it was his greatest pride. He knew everything about the show, what every singer was doing, and what every dancer was saying. Jazz Hoof was just like Crownpiece in that regard. So why would he want to ruin it?

But as she trotted back up to the stage to find him, Songbird heard a strange noise coming from the costume room. It was muffled by the sounds of music blasting onstage, but it was unmistakable. Somepony was ripping fabric!

As Songbird turned the corner and entered the room, she couldn't believe what she saw. Everypony's costumes, besides Rara's, were on the floor in a heap, ripped and cut beyond recognition! There was rainbow glitter in little piles everywhere, along with a red hoofsies stamp: the trademark signature logo of Countess Coloratura. Nopony but her had one of those stamps. Maybe Ritzy Rose and Jazz Hoof had been right about Rara all along.

Songbird Serenade snatched the hoofsies stamp and took off to alert Jazz Hoof. As Songbird replayed the scene in her head, there was only one conclusion she kept coming to: that her friend Countess Coloratura was trying to sabotage her competition and end the Glammys, once and for all.

The facts were all there—Songbird just didn't want to believe them.

CHAPTER FIFTEEN

By the time the big night had finally arrived, everypony had managed to recover from the costume attack. It was all thanks to the emergency sewing help from Rarity, her former intern Charity Sweetmint, and her good friend Ms. Pommel. All three designers called in extra seamstress friends to get the job done and had miraculously finished repairing everything earlier that afternoon. Jazz Hoof had declared it a "Musical Menagerie Miracle."

Despite the upset, most of the nominees found themselves looking forward to the evening of partying, performing, and finally finding out the winners of the awards. Pinkie Pie and Songbird Serenade were not among them. Why had Lyra and Bon Bon ever thought that they could pass this task off to a party planner and a pop singer?

Instead of feeling nervicited for their performance, they were sick with stress over their potentially failed mission. They had a main suspect, but still no Pondora Box or clear answers as to why Countess Coloratura would want to destroy the awards. And every time they tried to talk to her, she disappeared and retreated to her hotel room.

"Here goes nothing!" Pinkie Pie nudged Songbird and they stepped out of their carriage and onto the pink carpet. Suddenly, a friendly face popped up and made them momentarily forget their dilemma.

"Good evening, fine fillies!" Cheese Sandwich did a little bow and gave a wink. He looked dapper in his pink suit and red bow tie. "You're looking swell."

"Thank you, Mr. Sandwich." Songbird nodded and her sparkly bow caught the light. "I didn't know you'd be here, but I'm glad to see you again."

"Me too!" Pinkie Pie chirped. "Whatcha doin' here, Cheese?"

Cheese let out a belly laugh. "Good one, Pinkie. Thanks for asking Countess Coloratura to invite me. It's so rare that I get invited

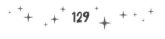

to a party I didn't plan! This must be what it feels like to be a normal pony."

"But I didn't ask Rara to invite you."

"Wait…" Cheese furrowed his brow, and reached into his pocket and procured two slips of purple paper. "She didn't send me this invitation?"

The invitation was hastily hoofwritten. The writing looked familiar, but it definitely was not Coloratura's. But there was a red hoofsies stamp at the bottom, and she was the only pony with one of those. It was puzzling. Pinkie Pie was trying to wrap her mind around it, when a line of thirty stallions in white tuxedos broke through the bustling pink-carpet crowd.

"Move aside!" barked a security pony. "Ballot boxes coming through!" Each of the stallions held a shining silver box with intricate crosshatch designs engraved into them.

Songbird and Pinkie Pie gasped and immediately looked at each other in shock. Those ballot boxes looked identical to the picture of the Pondora Box!

"Follow. Those. Boxes," Pinkie urged Songbird through her gritted, toothy smile. "Sorry, Cheese! Catch you later!" Songbird managed to push through the throngs of fancy ponies complimenting one another's gowns, but a perfectly polished white hoof stopped Pinkie Pie from following.

"Pinkie Pie, I'm delighted that you asked me to sew you a pink-carpet look along with the one for Songbird," Rarity cooed in the voice she reserved for formal occasions. She was wearing a gold-sequined gown that almost made her look like a giant Glammy statuette. Her purple mane was done up in a cascading-curl style.

"Finishing both garments was quite the time crunch, but if I do say so myself...you both look utterly divine." Rarity stepped back to admire Pinkie Pie's ensemble, which consisted of a black gown with a huge pink bow on the back, identical to Songbird Serenade's.

"Oh, thanks!" Pinkie Pie felt the dress was a bit much, but it did make her feel fuzzy-wuzzy warm that Rarity was so happy. Now if only her dear friend would take a hint and continue this conversation later. "I really gotta go—"

"It was so lucky that I was ahead of schedule, or Charity Sweetmint and I couldn't have repaired all those costumes." Rarity fanned herself as she remembered the destruction. She was flustered even imagining a tiny rip in one of her priceless dresses, let alone a bunch of them being torn to shreds. "It was horrifying."

While Pinkie Pie reassured her frantic friend and tried to break away, Songbird stuck to the plan and forged ahead. She waved to a few important ponies, weaving through the party with relative ease. Like a secret agent's sunglasses, Songbird's bangs provided excellent cover for avoiding eye contact. When she was sure she wasn't being watched, Songbird slipped into the ballot room.

Her heart began to thump rapidly inside her chest.

If anypony saw Songbird Serenade in there, they would automatically assume the worst— that she was trying to rig the outcome of the

awards. It could ruin her career! Songbird decided that, given the circumstances, it was a risk worth taking. She would save her friends and the Glammy attendees from that monster, no matter what it took. That is, if she could figure out which box it was first. How in Equestria was she going to tell the Pondora Box apart from all the others?

The thirty ballot boxes were placed on long tables along the perimeter of the room, along with the actual Glammy statuettes in neat rows beside them. They were identical. Whoever had stolen the box from Lyra and Bon Bon had managed to re-create the exact look of it for all the ballot boxes.

If she opened any of them, Songbird was going to be in big trouble. Either they would announce the winner of a category or they would release a terrifying mystery creature. She was trying to riddle out what her options were, when she heard her name.

"Songbird Serenade!" somepony shouted from outside the door. "Songbird?" Crownpiece leaned her head inside. True to her name, she was all gussied up for the big event and wearing a crown made of pretty bronze stars.

"Oh, it's just you." Songbird Serenade felt relief wash over her. She'd almost been caught!

Crownpiece raised an eyebrow and stepped into the doorway, her frame cast in silhouette. "Uhh…what are you doing?"

"Just admiring the new ballot boxes…" Songbird lied. "They're so…unique this year, don't you think?"

"Sure, I guess," Crownpiece replied, scrunching up her muzzle. "But not nice enough to miss your Glammy performance. Come on! You were supposed to be in costume five minutes ago. The show is starting and you're on first."

CHAPTER SIXTEEN

The excitement of the evening was tangible, almost an audible buzz. Pinkie Pie peeked through the curtains to survey the scene. The Stables Center was packed to the gills with ponies dressed in their fanciest clothing from all over Equestria, eager to see their favorite stars win awards and perform their latest hit songs live. Everypony was trying to guess who would win Pop Pony of the Year.

"Eez definitely going to bee Songbird Serenade to win Pop Pony!" guessed the famous photographer Photo Finish in her thick accent. "She 'az very nice voice and bold styles!"

"Personally, I've got my bits on Feather Bangs," said her friend and fashion designer Hoity Toity. He pushed down his purple aviator sunglasses and raised his eyebrows. "The fillies just *adore* him. And they have *major* influence. Never underestimate the fillies."

"I don't care who wins, as long as what they're wearing is fabulous," chimed in Dandy Grandeur from the row behind them. He was sporting his best fuzzy-necked vest and tie for the event. "You know?"

"Oh, it will be, darling," Rarity assured him. "Don't you fret." She imagined the moment when Songbird Serenade trotted up to accept the award wearing the gown she'd designed, and began to beam with pride. "Besides, I hear Jazz Hoof always puts on such a show. I can't wait to see what spectacles he's got in store for us!"

Little did they know that backstage it was already a sight to behold: It was utter chaos. The nominees were frantically trying to change their outfits and prepare to perform, while the stagehooves pushed the massive menagerie sets into order for seamless transitions. Pinkie Pie bounced up and down the hallways, searching for Songbird.

"There you are!" Pinkie Pie cheered as Songbird came galloping in, still pinning the pink bow to the back of her head. She'd just barely made it out of her dress and into her costume.

Pinkie Pie adjusted her own black top and

Songbird wig. "So, did you find the Pondora Box?! Please oh please oh please—"

"No," Songbird lamented as she picked up her microphone from a table of equipment. "The boxes are identical. Whoever did this really thought this scheme through. Now every time somepony opens a box onstage to read the winner of a category, they could be facing a terrible beast."

Pinkie Pie gulped. This was not how she'd imagined Glammy night going. She'd pictured sparkling apple juice and parties, not being on alert for scary monsters. There was nothing they could do now but keep their eyes open.

"Songbird Serenade—you're up!" A stage manager galloped over to Songbird and Pinkie with an angry expression on her face. "We're already behind schedule. We need you both to take your places, *now.*" Songbird and Pinkie gave each other a hoof-bump and galloped to their starting positions.

The stage was pitch-black as Songbird trilled out the opening notes to her song. *"Ohhhh, I've got strong hooves and a crystal heeaaaart..."* Her hauntingly beautiful voice echoed through the Stables Center.

A lone spotlight illuminated Pinkie Pie and she began her dance. She leaped across the stage with ease, her nerves having completely abandoned her in the wake of trying to solve the mystery. It was magic.

And it would have been perfect if Pinkie Pie hadn't spotted Crownpiece in the audience, carrying a silver box. The Unicorn kept looking over her shoulder, as if she was nervous that somepony would stop her. Right away, Pinkie Pie knew that it was the box she had been searching for. Pinkie Pie hoped Songbird Serenade would understand if she went off routine a bit. Because before she could stop herself, Pinkie Pie was diving off the stage and into the audience.

"*Geronimoooo!*" Pinkie Pie couldn't help shouting, just like Cheese Sandwich would have. She tackled the assistant in a blur of black and fuchsia, and quickly grabbed the box. Songbird kept singing, and everypony watched the scene unfolding in the audience with curiosity. Was it part of the show? One never truly knew with Songbird Serenade and her taste for performance art, so nopony got up to stop the altercation.

"What do you think you're doing?!" Crown-piece barked, trying to wrestle the box back. "This is the ballot box for Pop Pony of the Year!"

"No, it's not!" Pinkie Pie yelled. "It's a Pon-dora Box! It's dangerous! There's a *monsteeeeeer* in *theeeeere!*" Crownpiece dove for the box, and both ponies crashed down onto the floor. Pinkie landed on her stomach with a *splat!* The box was just beyond her forehoof's reach. She scooted and stretched. . . .

"Whoaaaa, I've got strong hooves and a crystal heart . . . but your magic spells might be too smart! I'm like a shiny relic, a piece of art!" Songbird belted out onstage, watching Pinkie and Crownpiece roll around from underneath her choppy bangs.

Crownpiece hopped to her hooves and snatched the box. "Look, if you wanna see,

I'll show you what's inside!" she shouted over the music. Then Crownpiece placed her hoof on the lock and twisted it back and forth in a series of complicated movements. Where had she learned to do that?

As the lid flipped open, a brilliant blast of red light shot up from inside the box. A gust of wind swirled around Crownpiece, causing her golden mane to fly up like the Mane-iac. Her face looked spooky, illuminated from below with the red tint, but she did not look powerful. She seemed...scared?

That couldn't be a sign of good things to come.

Crownpiece quickly dropped the box to the floor, but it was too late. The spell had been cast. The breeze picked up, and wind whipped through the rows of seated audience ponies and formed a small tornado in the center of the aisle. Masses of iridescent glitter soared from the box and up into the air above the ponies, creating an effect that erred more on the side of lovely than terrifying. *"Ooooh..."* the audience cooed in wonder as the glitter danced to Songbird's voice.

BOOM! A loud noise resonated through the theater as the glitter sucked itself into the aisle. When the cloud settled, a giant figure made entirely out of glitter particles emerged. Its glowing red eyes shone like lasers as it stomped through the aisles, swinging its massive fists at the audience and growling.

"Ahhhhh!" the ponies cried out. "What is that thing?!"

"I don't know," Dandy Grandeur whimpered. "But it seems angry, you know?"

"Songbird!" Pinkie Pie shouted from the seats. "We have to stop the monster!"

"It's a Glitter Golem!" shouted Lyra, wearing a mask and appearing out of nowhere and doing a barrel roll into the aisle. A disguised Bon Bon followed, pulling a small gold contraption from the pocket of her black waistcoat. "Stay back, everypony. We have to calm it down so we can catch it!"

Onstage, Songbird Serenade stopped singing "Crystal Heart," captivated by the sight of the creature ambling through the theater, clawing at everything. Its body sparkled like a million beautiful diamonds, but it sounded ugly—like an Ursa Major with a thorn in its paw. She wanted to do something to help, too, but what? It felt like her hooves were glued to the floor.

And then Songbird began to hum a low,

smooth lullaby. The Glitter Golem stopped in its tracks. It spun around, entranced by the notes of the song, and began to walk toward Songbird.

"Keep singing!" shouted Bon Bon. "It's working!"

"*Traaa-la-la, hmmmmm mmmm, la-laaaa . . .*" Songbird cooed. With each step the Glitter Golem took toward the stage, more glitter fell from the creature's limbs. By the time it reached Songbird, it was just a faint translucent shimmer. As Songbird sang the last of the notes, the beast had completely disappeared.

The only remnants of it were the little piles of glitter across the stage. Songbird sighed with relief and spoke into her microphone. "And that, fillies and gentlecolts, brings us to intermission! Please escort yourselves outside for a refreshment."

"*WAHOOOOO!* That was amazing, Song-bird!" Pinkie Pie squealed from the audience, bouncing into the air. "You did it!"

Pinkie had never seen a better performance in her entire life.

CHAPTER
SEVENTEEN

There was only one pony who had full access to the entire Stables Center and who had a hoof in everything with the awards. One pony who was excellent at planning, so good that she could be somepony's assistant and execute a plot to destroy a pop singer's reputation at the same time. One pony who was sneaky enough to steal a boxed magical monster and place it among the ballots. Finally, it all made sense: the destroyed sets, the ruined costumes, and the random piles of mysterious glitter. Why hadn't they seen it before?

"I know who tried to sabotage the Glammy Awards!" Pinkie Pie shouted, bringing everypony's excited chatter to an abrupt end. Pinkie Pie paused as if she were going to read the winner of a Glammy Award. "It was *CROWNPIECE*!" She pointed at the stunned assistant.

Everypony gasped. The nominees and their dancers shuffled their hooves and stepped away from the Unicorn. Crownpiece was left standing in the middle of the circle, eyes wide with faux innocence. "That's not true!"

Nopony could believe it. Especially Songbird Serenade, who looked incredibly hurt. Had her own assistant really duped her this entire time?

"But—but…that's impossible," Ritzy Rose stammered, crestfallen. "I'm positive that it was Ra—"

"That's what she wanted you to think…" Pinkie Pie explained. She trotted over to Ritzy and put a hoof around her shoulders like they were old pals. "Ritzy Rose, you were sure you were going to win a Glammy last year. Who stole the show instead?"

"Countess Coloratura!" Ritzy Rose proclaimed, sticking her muzzle in the air. Moonlight Melody nodded in support. "That's what I'm trying to tell you."

Now that Pinkie was rolling with her theories, she couldn't stop. Pinkie Pie trotted over to Jazz Hoof, who was dressed in a royal-blue suit with a neon yellow cravat. "And, Jazz Hoof, who complained to the Glammy producers to have you replaced as the show's director and host?"

Jazz Hoof scoffed and closed his eyes in disgust. "My sources have informed me that it was definitely Countess Coloratura."

"And Countess Coloratura was the only nominee who did not have her sets and costumes destroyed by a gigantic glitter monster!" whined Jewel Tone.

Daisy Chain jutted out her bottom lip and nodded. "Yeah!"

Pinkie Pie nodded wisely. "So all signs point to Coloratura...or do they?"

Everypony turned to look at Rara's reaction. But the pop star didn't say a thing—she simply burst into a fit of laughter. Once Rara composed herself, she shrugged with an apologetic smile. "I'm sorry for laughing. It's just that I would never do any of that. It's all so preposterous!" Rara paused and considered again. "Somepony must be really upset with me if they would spread those rumors and try to frame me for ruining sets."

"Exactly! Which brings me to my next point...the motive." Pinkie Pie spun around dramatically and pointed at Crownpiece. "Tell us, Crownpiece, who fired your *brother*—SVENGALLOP?! It was Countess Coloratura...was it not?!"

Rara blushed at the mention of the awkward exchange with her former manager. The two had had very different ideas about how Countess Coloratura should run her career. Crownpiece's face fell as the realization dawned on her.

Crownpiece went pale. "H-h-h-how did you know Svengallop is my brother?"

"Easy-peasy. I just put hoofwriting and hoofwriting together..." revealed Pinkie Pie. She held up a slip of purple notebook paper. "Before the show, my friend Cheese showed me this invitation, signed *Countess Coloratura*. It even has a hoofsies stamp on it! A stamp that only Rara—or somepony who worked for her—would have access to."

Pinkie paced back and forth. The ponies were rapt with attention. "I knew I recognized it from somewhere. Crownpiece dropped a piece of paper during rehearsal one day. She was always dropping papers, so I scooped this one up to help her out. I tried to return it, but she was busy with assistant duties, as always.

And when I compared the papers, it was the same writing."

"What?" Crownpiece scoffed. "That doesn't prove anything."

But Pinkie Pie was unshaken. She had all the answers. "You knew Songbird and I were close to discovering the truth about your plan to ruin Rara's career, so you invited my friend Cheese Sandwich to distract me away from the trail!"

Songbird Serenade couldn't take it anymore. She felt so betrayed. She had put her trust into Crownpiece, but she was only pretending to be her friend. "Well...did you do it?" she asked sadly.

"It's true!" Crownpiece wailed, collapsing to the floor. "All of it!" The pony stifled a few sobs, then composed herself and stood up. "I

wanted to help my brother, Svengallop. He was so upset after the way she tossed him aside so carelessly, so he was determined to ruin Rara's career. At first he just wanted to ruin some of her costumes, but then a pony at a magic shop sold him this box. The pony said that it held a spell that would make it look like there was a fearsome beast."

"What?!" Rara was already in shock from the confession, but then she saw Svengallop himself emerge from the shadows of the curtains. His poufy pink coif and blue waistcoat was unmistakable. He was red with embarrassment, but somehow he still had a bad attitude.

"That's enough, Crownpiece." Svengallop looked annoyed at having to explain himself. "It was me. Are you happy? *I* devised the plan to frame Rara on the biggest night of the year," Svengallop admitted with a sneer. "And I didn't want anypony to suspect me, so I made my sister pretend to be your assistant, Songbird. It was the only way to put everything in place before tonight."

Pinkie Pie's mind was officially blown. She'd just been going on wild theory, connecting dots all willy-nilly. But here Svengallop was, actually confessing to everything! *I really should be a detective*, she thought proudly.

Crownpiece sniffed and pushed her golden mane away from her face to look straight at Songbird. "I'm so sorry I put you through all of this."

"What you did was wrong." Songbird gave her a little smile. "But in the wise words of my friend Rara: 'You are just a pony, and you make mistakes from time to time.' You were

just trying to help your brother." Songbird put her hoof on Crownpiece's shoulder. "I'm sure if you both apologize to everypony here, we can find it in our hearts to forgive you."

Much to Crownpiece's surprise, everypony onstage was nodding, even Countess Coloratura. Svengallop looked up from his hooves with a hint of hope. "Really?" Crownpiece asked with tears welling up in her eyes. "You'd all do that?"

Crownpiece didn't want to quit working for Songbird Serenade. Even though she'd been a part of Svengallop's ridiculous plan, she'd grown to love being around all these ponies, anticipating their needs and helping them. For once in her life, Crownpiece had found something she actually liked to do. "And I could keep being your assistant?"

"Of course!" Songbird lifted up her bangs and gave Crownpiece a little wink. "*If* you let me write a song about all this...." Everypony laughed. Songbird Serenade sure knew how to make light of any situation.

"Okay, everypony! Enough warm fuzzies!" Jazz Hoof called out, trotting to the front of the curtain and facing the singers. "Now, we've got a show to finish!"

CHAPTER EIGHTEEN

Once the glittery mess had been cleaned up and the confused audience corralled back inside to their seats, the Glammy Awards went off without another hitch. It turned out to be the beautiful night of music and celebration that everypony had been hoping for.

Each nominee had the chance to perform his or her Musical Menagerie songs (with a bit of residual glitter) to much applause. The long hours they'd logged in rehearsal were evident. Each performance was stunning in its own way, and still appeared as a cohesive art piece. Nopony was quite sure whether the Glitter Golem had been a fancy magical effect for the purpose of the show or if it was indeed real. But it didn't matter either way.

By the end of the show, Jazz Hoof was beaming with pride at his masterpiece. And though Pinkie Pie couldn't speak for anypony in charge, she was pretty sure he was here to stay as host and director for many years to come.

After the performances, it was finally time to announce the awards winners of the evening. The silver ballot boxes worked perfectly, revealing winners just as they were supposed to—no more monsters. Ritzy Rose even took home her first Glammy, for Best Live Summer Sun Celebration Performance. And Hoity Toity was very smug about the fact that Feather Bangs shocked everypony by sweeping many categories, boasting a rookie record of six awards by the end of the night. He wouldn't let Photo Finish hear the end of it.

Finally, it was the big moment. Pinkie Pie held her breath in giddy anticipation as Jazz Hoof trotted onstage with the last silver box. "And the Pop Pony of the Year is"—Jazz Hoof stomped his hooves on the ground and the audience followed along, creating a rumble that shook the walls—"Songbird Serenade!"

After the curtain had fallen, and the celebratory sparkling juice toasts had been made,

Songbird and Pinkie noticed Lyra and Bon Bon trying to slip out the backstage door without so much as a good-bye. Crownpiece was with the duo, but she was smiling, so everything seemed okay.

"Hey!" Pinkie Pie bounded over, Songbird in tow. "Where are you ponies going?! Party's just getting started!" Pinkie tried to pass them a glass of juice, but they held up their hooves in protest.

"Pinkie, Songbird—Operation Pondora was successful thanks to you two. But our work here is done," Bon Bon said with a slight nod, which was the unofficial salute of the agency. "And don't worry, we're just taking Crownpiece to S.M.I.L.E. hidequarters for some debriefing, and then she's free to come back and work as Songbird's assistant for as long as she likes."

Lyra nudged Pinkie with a laugh. "We can't

have anypony knowing how to steal and use a Pondora Box. That's top secret information!"

Pinkie furrowed her brow. "But Songbird and I know how to open it—"

"*Do* you?" Lyra said with a sly smirk as she opened a shiny compact mirror. The light caught in Pinkie's and Songbird's eyes. All of a sudden, things seemed very fuzzy.

Pinkie and Songbird found themselves standing by a doorway and staring at the handle.

"Uh...what were we talking about again...?" Pinkie Pie scratched her head and searched Songbird's face for clues.

"You know, it's the funniest thing. I don't remember...." Songbird mused. She stared at the door handle, but nothing came to mind. "How strange."

"Oh well! Guess it wasn't important." Pinkie

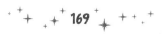

shrugged and giggled. Suddenly, a fun beat started blasting through the speakers. Pinkie couldn't help tapping her hoofs.

Songbird grinned. "Come on, Pinkie! They're playing our song!"

"You don't have to ask me twice!"

And with that, the two new pals headed back to rejoin the party and dance the night away like nopony was watching.

ON DVD 2/13!

SPRING INTO FRIENDSHI